BAD KITTY
SCAREDY-CAT

NICK BRUEL

A NEAL PORTER BOOK
ROARING BROOK PRESS
NEW YORK

For Jennie, Edward, Ridley, and Phoebe

Cataloging-in-Publication Data is on file at the Library of Congress

ISBN: 978-1-59643-978-8

Our books may be purchased in bulk for promotional, educational, or business use. Please
contact your local bookseller or the Macmillan Corporate and Premium Sales Department
at (800) 221-7945 ext. 5442 or by e-mail at MacmillanSpecialMarkets@macmillan.com.

First edition 2016
Printed in China by RR Donnelley Asia Printing Solutions Ltd., Dongguan City, Guangdong Province

1 3 5 7 9 10 8 6 4 2

She wasn't always a scaredy-cat.

She used to be . . .

But then, one dark and foggy night, something terrible happened.

Out of the darkness and into her
doorway appeared the most horrible
and frightening creatures
Kitty had ever seen.

She saw . . .

AN **A**WFUL **A**LIEN   A **B**IZARRE **B**IGFOOT

A **C**REEPY
CLOWN   A **D**READFUL
DRAGON

A **Y**UCKY **Y**ETI!   AND A **Z**ANY **Z**OMBIE.

That's how she became a scaredy-cat.
That's how she became just a very, very,
scared, scared, **SCARED** little kitty.
Poor Kitty. Poor, poor Kitty.

But then . . .

OOPS! I DROPPED MY CANDY!

**That's when she saw it.
She saw . . .**

APPLES, **B**UBBLEGUM, **C**ANDY CORN, **D**RIED FRUIT, **E**NGLISH TOFFEE, **F**UDGE, **G**UMDROPS, **H**ARD CANDY, **I**TALIAN TRUFFLES, **J**ELLYBEANS, **K**IWI FRUIT, **L**OLLIPOPS, **M**ARSHMALLOWS,

Necklaces, **O**ranges, **P**retzels, **Q**uince candy, **R**aisins, **S**trawberry licorice, **T**affy, **U**nsalted nuts, **V**anilla cookies, **W**hite chocolate, wa**X** lips, **Y**ellow bananas, and **Z**oo animal crackers.

Kitty decided there and then that she would not be a scared, little kitty anymore. She decided she would be a BAD KITTY!

But not just any bad kitty—
she would be a very, very,
bad, bad, BAD kitty.

She . . .

HOORAY FOR KITTY!

All by herself, Kitty managed to chase those horrible creatures back out into the night!

Kitty decided there and then that she would NEVER be a scaredy-cat again.

Never.